Both BARBARA BAKER and NOLA
LANGNER MALONE have had
plenty of experience living in
large families. Barbara Baker
is one of many children, and
Nola Malone is the mother of
five.

Ms. Baker is the author of
*Digby and Kate, Digby and
Kate Again,* and *Third Grade
Is Terrible.*

Ms. Malone has illustrated
thirty books, fifteen of which
she wrote herself.

Keep me clean

Please Don't
Handle Me
With Soiled
Hands.

N-O Spells NO!

by Barbara Baker

and Nola Langner Malone

DUTTON CHILDREN'S BOOKS

NEW YORK

for Pat Costa

B.A.B.

for all children, everywhere,
who hate the word N-O

N.L.M.

Library of Congress Cataloging-in-Publication Data

Baker, Barbara, date.
  N-O spells no / by Barbara Baker and Nola Langner Malone. —
1st ed.
    p. cm.
  Summary: Five episodes occurring over a weekend about Walter and his
younger sister, Annie.
  ISBN 0-525-44639-7
  [1. Brothers and sisters—Fiction.] I. Malone, Nola Langner.
II. Title.
PZ7.B16922Naac   1990
  [Fic]—dc20   90-19714
                                                          CIP
                                                           AC

Published in the United States by
Dutton Children's Books,
a division of Penguin Books USA Inc.

Printed in U.S.A.   First Edition
10 9 8 7 6 5 4 3 2 1

 *Saturday Morning*

Annie and Walter were watching television.

Annie moved closer to the TV.

"Why?" said Walter. "It's just a dumb baby show."

"It is not," said Annie. "I like it. And it's my turn to choose the program."

She looked at Walter. "But if you *really* don't want to watch it . . . I'll play Star Blast with you, instead." Annie was dying to try Walter's new game.

"N-O spells no," said Walter. He turned back to the TV.

Their mother came into the living room. "I'm going out shopping," she said. "And I want you to clean your rooms."

"No," said their mother. She switched off the TV. "You've been sitting here all morning. And your rooms look like pigpens."

Walter waited until the front door closed. Then he turned the TV back on.

You're going to get it.

Annie went to her room.

She started to work.
She made her bed,

picked up her toys,

hung up some clothes,
and put her shoes away.
It took a long time.

She even cleaned under her bed. She
found

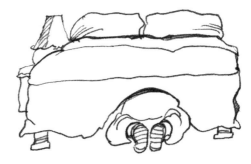

 a missing sneaker,

 her blue bead necklace,

a book,

and her Wonder Woman cape.

She put the cape on and looked in her mirror.

"Ha!" said Walter. "Fat chance."

Annie jumped.

The front door banged.

"Oh, no! It's Mom," said Walter. He hadn't even started to clean his room. He knew he was in trouble.

Annie almost said no, but then she
thought about Star Blast. She picked up
the book she had found.

I have a plan.
Put this on
my bookshelf.

So Walter did.

Walter didn't answer. He looked at Annie.

Walter?

"He didn't do it yet," said Annie. "Because I had a great idea. First Walter helped me clean *my* room. And now *I'm* going to help Walter."

Their mother looked surprised. "I'm glad to see you working together for a change," she said. Then she went back down the hall.

15

"Well," said Annie, "if *that's* the way you feel, you can clean your own big mess."

Just then the doorbell rang.

Annie, it's Jill and Sarah.

The Spooky Voice

Annie's mother came into the living room. The girls were watching TV.

It stopped raining. Why don't you girls go outside?

We don't want to go out. It's too wet.

"All right," said her mother. "But find something else to do in here. The TV needs a rest."

Walter came into the room. He had a
pile of books and pencils and paper.
He sat down on the couch.

"Too bad if we do," said Annie. "You can go in your own *nice clean* room, you know."

Walter stayed where he was.

"Annie," said Jill, "could we borrow your brother's Star Blast game?"

"*No,*" said Walter. "You can*not* borrow it. So don't even ask."

We can play Chinese Checkers since Walter is so stingy and won't let us play with his game.

Annie set up the Chinese Checkers on the floor.

They began to play. Annie went first.
They all took turns.

They played until Sarah won.

"I don't feel like playing anymore," said Annie. "Let's take a break."

Annie and her friends went into the kitchen.

Walter followed them into the kitchen.

Annie put cookies on a big plate. Walter
got the milk out of the refrigerator.

Walter grabbed some cookies and sat
down at the table.

I have an idea. Let's make a house in the living room We can use the folding table and a blanket.

Annie went to get a blanket while Jill
and Sarah put the table up.

When the house was ready, they all
crawled under.

It's private in here. Walter can't bother us.
That's what you think.
THUMP
THUMP!

"Go away, Walter. We know it's you,"
said Annie.

The spooky voice moaned and groaned.

"I thought I told you to get lost," said
Annie.

Jill and Sarah giggled. Jill poked Annie. "I have an idea to make him go away," she whispered. Then she said in a loud voice:

"I think your brother is s-o-o-o cute," said Jill.

The spooky voice stopped moaning and groaning.

"I think he's the *cutest* boy I know," said Jill. "Maybe he can be my *boyfriend*."

Annie peeked out of the house.

"He's leaving," she said. "Jill's plan worked."

The three friends shook hands.

"Now," said Annie, "help me think of a plan to get hold of Star Blast."

Star Blast

Annie and Walter were alone. Their mother was still next door, and Jill and Sarah had gone home.

"I'm going out," said Walter.

I'll be back after the game.

Annie waited until the front door slammed.

She tiptoed up the stairs to Walter's
bedroom.

Star Blast was on Walter's highest shelf.
"He thinks I won't be able to reach it,"
Annie said to herself. "I'll show him."

She saw Walter's desk chair.

Annie dragged the chair across the floor to the bookshelf. Then she climbed up on it and reached.

Her fingers just touched the edge of the box.

She stood on her toes and stretched.
Now her fingers got a grip on the sides of
the box. She pulled. The box was heavy.

She pulled harder. The box began to
slip.

Annie jumped down from the chair. She had a terrible feeling in her stomach. What would Walter do to her?

She opened the box.

Rocks! The box was filled with rocks.

A piece of paper was taped to one of the rocks.

Good Night

Annie and Walter were in their beds.
But Annie wasn't tired. She was thinking.

It had been hard,
but she had put the
box back up on the
shelf in Walter's room.

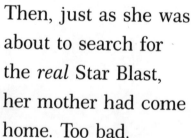

Then, just as she was
about to search for
the *real* Star Blast,
her mother had come
home. Too bad.

Annie sat up and tapped quietly on her
wall. Walter's bed was on the other side.

She listened—nothing.
She tapped louder.

Walter banged once on the wall.
Annie giggled.

"Be quiet, you two. It's late," called their
mother from the living room.

44

Annie was quiet for one minute. Then she stepped carefully out of bed. She put her blanket over her head and tiptoed down the hall to Walter's room.

Walter sat up. He took his pillow and threw it at Annie as hard as he could.

"Shhh," said Annie. "Do you want Mom to hear?"

Annie was too late.

"In *here*?" said her mother.

I guess I made a mistake.

"Wait just a minute," said her mother. "I don't think you need a drink of water. I think you both need another bedtime story."

"We *do*?" said Annie.

"Once upon a time," her mother started, "there was a little boy and a little girl. They were brother and sister."

"It was late at night," she went on, "but the boy and the girl would not go to sleep.

The boy and the girl banged on walls. They yelled and shouted.

The girl even got out of her bed and went into her brother's room. This boy and girl made their mother very, *very* angry."

Walter pulled his covers up and closed
his eyes.

Annie ran past her mother, down the
hall, and into her room. She jumped into
bed.

Soon Annie and Walter were fast asleep.

Little Martin

The next morning was sunny. Annie wanted to go to Jill's house. Walter wanted to play ball.

Their mother had a different plan. "Aunt Lucy is coming to visit. And she's bringing little Martin."

The doorbell rang. Annie and Walter groaned. It was Aunt Lucy and little Martin.

Martin ran right past Annie and Walter.
"Oh, isn't that sweet?" said Aunt Lucy.
"Martin wants to play."
Annie and Walter raced after Martin.

First Martin ran into Annie's room. He grabbed her Chinese Checkers box.

She tried to take it away from him.
Martin pulled.
The lid flew off the box.

Marbles rolled everywhere.

Walter helped Annie pick up the marbles.

Annie and Walter heard something. They ran down the hall.

They found Martin in the bathroom. He was dropping something into the toilet. "Bye-bye!" sang Martin.

"Martin," said Annie, "what did you flush?"

"All gone," said Martin. He laughed.

"*What's* all gone?" said Walter.

But Martin wouldn't say.

The soap was missing. So were the toothbrushes and the cap to the toothpaste.

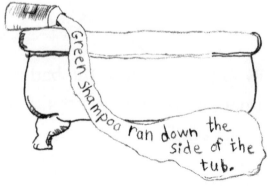

Green Shampoo ran down the side of the tub.

Martin ran into Walter's room.

Martin dropped Walter's homework. He ran out of the room, down the hall, and back into Annie's room.

Martin reached for the fishbowl.

Annie grabbed Martin. Walter grabbed
the fishbowl. The fish sloshed back and
forth. Martin tried to bite Annie's hand.

Annie and Walter grabbed
Martin by the
arms.

They
dragged him
to the living room.

"Oh, there you are," said Aunt Lucy.
"Was Martin a good boy?"

"We'll have to come again soon, for a longer visit," said Aunt Lucy.

Martin smiled like an angel.

Annie and Walter looked at the ceiling.

Annie sighed. "Just think what it would be like if Martin was our *brother*," she said.

Walter thought about it. "We could take turns sitting on him," he said.

Annie laughed. "Or maybe we could get little handcuffs or . . .

You know, Walter, sometimes I'm glad *you're* my brother."

Walter got up and walked out of the room. He came back with a box in his hands.

"Star Blast," said Annie. "What are you going to do with it?"

"Uh . . ." said Walter. "You want to play?"

"Really?" Annie couldn't believe her ears.

"You're a lot nicer than Martin," said Walter.

Then Annie and Walter settled down to a good long game of Star Blast.